MySELF Bookshelf

Lulu the Shy Piglet

By SoYun Jeong

Illustrated by Laura Orsolini

Language Arts Consultant: Joy Cowley

NORWOOD HOUSE PRESS

Chicago, Illinois

DEAR CAREGIVER MySELF ▮ ▮▮ Bookshelf is a series of books that support children's social emotional learning. SEL has been proven to promote not only the development of self-awareness, responsibility, and positive relationships, but also academic achievement.

Current research reveals that the part of the brain that manages emotion is directly connected to the part of the brain that is used in cognitive tasks, such as: problem solving, logic, reasoning, and critical thinking—all of which are at the heart of learning.

SEL is also directly linked to what are referred to as 21st Century Skills: collaboration, communication, creativity, and critical thinking. MySELF Bookshelf offers an early start that will help children build the competencies for success in school and life.

In these delightful books, young children practice early reading skills while learning how to manage their own feelings and how to be considerate of other perspectives. Each book focuses on aspects of SEL that help children develop social competence that will benefit them in their relationships with others as well as in their school success. The charming characters in the stories model positive traits such as: responsibility, goal setting, determination, patience, and celebrating differences. At the end of each story, you will find a letter that highlights the positive traits and an activity or discussion to help your child apply SEL to his or her own life.

Above all, the most important part of the reading experience is to have fun and enjoy it!

Sincerely,

Shannon Cannon

Shannon Cannon, Ph.D.
Literacy and SEL Consultant

Norwood House Press • P.O. Box 316598 • Chicago, Illinois 60631
For more information about Norwood House Press please visit our website at www.norwoodhousepress.com or call 866-565-2900.

Shannon Cannon—Literacy and SEL Consultant
Joy Cowley—English Language Arts Consultant
Mary Lindeen—Consulting Editor

Library of Congress Cataloging-in-Publication Data
    Jeong, SoYun.
    Lulu the shy piglet / by SoYun Jeong ; illustrated by Laura Orsolini.
        pages cm. -- (MySELF bookshelf)
    "Social and emotional learning concepts include fear of speaking to others and learning how to make friends." Summary: Lulu the piglet is very shy and does not like to sing or speak in public, but a mouse overhears her singing in the barn and offers to help Lulu overcome her shyness by arranging for a performance with their friends.
    ISBN 978-1-59953-645-3 (library edition : alk. paper) -- ISBN 978-1-60357-667-3 (ebook)
    [1. Bashfulness--Fiction. 2. Singing--Fiction. 3. Pigs--Fiction. 4. Mice--Fiction. 5. Domestic animals--Fiction.] I. Orsolini, Laura, illustrator II. Title. PZ7.J457Lul 2014
    [E]--dc23
                                        2014009392

Manufactured in the United States of America in Stevens Point, Wisconsin.
252N—072014

Lulu the piglet was kind.

Lulu the piglet was a good singer.

But Lulu was so shy

that her voice was a tiny squeak.

Lulu's cheeks turned red.
She ran into the house
and sat all by herself.
Poor Lulu!

Lulu's favorite place
was an old empty barn.
When Lulu was there,
she felt happy and calm.
She could sing a happy song
because no one was listening.

Well, almost no one.

9

A little mouse said, "Wow!
You sing like a star!
You should be on a stage!"

Lulu's heart jumped
and her face turned red.

The mouse said to her,
"Your cheeks are on fire,
but that is okay.
Just keep on singing."

But it wasn't okay.
Lulu ran away.

The next day,
Lulu was walking along
with her head down,
when someone ran up to her.

"Hi, again!"
It was that mouse.

Lulu was still embarrassed
so she pretended not to hear.

The mouse shouted at her,
"Let's be friends!"

The mouse put black sunglasses
on Lulu the piglet.
"This is a friendship gift," he said.
"Do you feel less shy?
Do you feel more brave?
That's because these glasses
get rid of shyness."

"Oh! Really?" said Lulu.

Lulu walked around the farm.
She didn't hang her head.
She looked at the other animals
and they looked at her.
She even smiled at them.
She felt very confident
with her special glasses.

Lulu's voice got louder
and her face was not as red.

"You did it! You are so brave!"
said the mouse.

Lulu was so pleased
that she sang for her friend.

The mouse clapped and clapped.
"Tomorrow you can sing
for all the farm animals."

Lulu smiled and nodded.

Lulu was very pleased
that she was going to sing.
But she tripped over Miss Sheep
and her black sunglasses flew off.

They landed on the ground
just as Mr. Ox stepped backwards.

"What's the matter, Lulu?"
asked the mouse.

Lulu sobbed, "I can't sing today.
My glasses are broken."

The mouse said gently,
"Lulu, look at your reflection.
Nothing has changed.
The voice that got louder is yours.
The beautiful singing is yours.
It's not the sunglasses, Lulu.
It is you!
You don't need the glasses."

23

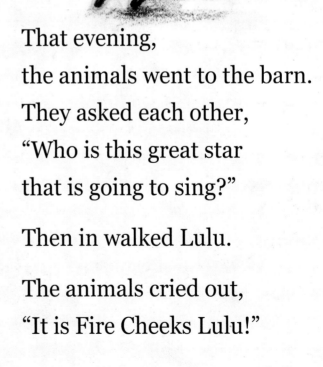

That evening,
the animals went to the barn.
They asked each other,
"Who is this great star
that is going to sing?"

Then in walked Lulu.

The animals cried out,
"It is Fire Cheeks Lulu!"

Lulu said in a shaky voice,
"I'm very nervous
but I will do my best."

The animals cheered
and that made her feel better.
She began to sing.

Her voice was beautiful.
Everyone wanted her to sing
over and over again.

26

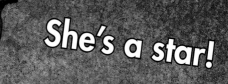

She's a star!

Beautiful!

27

Dear Lulu,

Today you were fantastic!
You are the star of our farm.
We think you are amazing
because you sing well.
You are even more amazing
because you overcame your shyness
to sing for all the animals.
You don't need dark sunglasses anymore.
If you get nervous, be nervous.
If you feel shy, be shy.
Don't run away and hide.
Be what you are.
When you get courage,
you shine like the treasure
that you really are.

Your friend,
Mouse

SOCIAL AND EMOTIONAL LEARNING FOCUS

Shy Personality

Lulu thought that the sunglasses helped her overcome her shyness to be able to sing in front of others. However, she learned that her talent is like a gift that could be shared. When she realized that her singing was like a treasure, she let it shine for all to see.

Sometimes we need help remembering the treasures we have and can share with others. You can make a treasure chest to remind you of the gifts you have. Draw the shape to the right on a piece of paper and cut it out to make a treasure chest. You can also use a shoe box if you have one. Now think of the talents or treasures that describe you. Decorate your chest and fill it with "coins" that remind you of your own treasures. You can use circles cut from paper, or any round objects as coins (for example, plastic bottle tops, or buttons). If you have craft supplies, you can add beads, gems or shiny stones and decorations to your chest and coins.

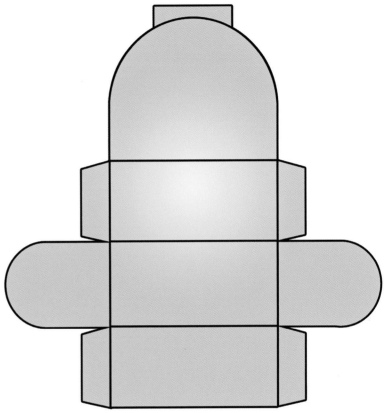

Reader's Theater

Reader's Theater is an interactive approach to reading that allows students to understand each story through dramatic interpretation. By involving students in reading, listening, and speaking activities, they provide an integrated approach for students to develop fluency and comprehension. A Reader's Theater edition of this book is available online. You can access the script by scanning the QR code to the right or visit our website at: http://www.norwoodhousepress.com/lulutheshypiglet.aspx